Garlunk

Helen Cresswell

Illustrated by Margaret Chamberlain

CAMBRIDGE
UNIVERSITY PRESS

FOR BEN AND GABRIELLA

Cambridge Reading

General Editors

Richard Brown
Kate Ruttle

Consultant Editor

Jean Glasberg

PUBLISHED BY THE PRESS SYNDICATE OF THE UNIVERSITY OF CAMBRIDGE
The Pitt Building, Trumpington Street, Cambridge CB2 1RP, United Kingdom

CAMBRIDGE UNIVERSITY PRESS
The Edinburgh Building, Cambridge CB2 2RU, United Kingdom
40 West 20th Street, New York, NY 10011-4211, USA
10 Stamford Road, Oakleigh, Melbourne 3166, Australia

First published 1998

Printed in the United Kingdom at the University Press, Cambridge

Typeset in Concorde

A catalogue record for this book is available from the British Library

ISBN 0 521 46890 6 paperback

CONTENTS

Chapter One   4

Chapter Two   14

Chapter Three   25

Chapter Four   37

Chapter Five   53

ONE

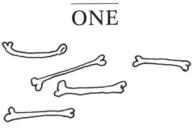

GARLUNK the giant sat in his cave half-way up the mountain. He had just woken up and kept yawning, huge red yawns.

He picked up a couple of old sheep bones and cracked them in two. He liked the sound they made. Crack!

Crack!

The bones would make good tooth-picks. He often got food stuck between his long yellow teeth. These days, that food was usually mutton. It was a very long time since Garlunk had eaten a small boy or girl. This was a pity, because this had always been his favourite meal.

Sometimes he boiled them. Sometimes he roasted them in his huge oven, with a few sacks of potatoes. But he wasn't fussy. Sometimes he had even eaten them raw.

There was no furniture in the cave, no table or chair. There was no mirror, either, and that was a good thing. Garlunk's face was ugly enough to crack any glass. He had piggy eyes and a knob of a nose and altogether too many teeth.

You wouldn't really expect a giant to have a looking-glass. Giants don't care a fig what they look like.

They don't have baths very often, either. When giants bath, they jump into a river or lake. They have never heard of soap. They don't care. The worse they look, the more they can frighten people. And the *smell*! The pong of a giant is enough to make you wish you'd been born without a nose.

But Garlunk never even looked at his own reflection in the mountain pools and lakes, never mind jumped into them. He was terrified of seeing himself. There was a very good reason for that.

Once, long ago, he had annoyed a wizard. That wizard lived in another cave further down the mountain. Like all good wizards and witches, he had a cat.

One day, as Garlunk went by, he had seen the wizard fast asleep with the cat curled up beside him. "That looks like a tasty snack!" said Garlunk to himself. And he had picked up the cat and popped it into his mouth, fur and all. Fur, eyes, teeth and claws – yuk!

As the cat went down Garlunk's throat, it had let out a screech –

"EEEEEECH!"

The wizard woke up, but it was too late. He was mad, he was furious, he was steaming at the ears. "I'll fix you!" he screamed. "I'll put a curse on you!"

And so he had. If ever Garlunk caught so much as a glimpse of himself, he would turn to stone. Pff! Just like that! No wonder Garlunk was terrified of mirrors and pools. And no wonder he had such a pong.

That spell had been made years and years ago – hundreds of years, thousands. And never once in all that time had Garlunk seen himself.

Giants in Wales live to a very old age. This is because they spend nearly all their time sleeping. They sometimes go to sleep and don't wake up for perhaps a hundred years. Then they get up, feeling very hungry.

Garlunk had been asleep for a hundred and two years, seven months and three

days. He was very, very hungry. He was ravenous. He could eat a whole flock of sheep. (It is lucky that giants sleep so much, or there would be no sheep left in Wales.) "Food!" he growled.

People in the valley below thought they could hear the distant rumble of thunder. They ran out into their gardens. "Better take the washing in!" they said. "Funny – it never said anything about storms in the forecast!"

Rumble

"My beard! Where's my shears?"

While giants sleep, their beards go on growing. They silently grow, inch by inch, whisker by whisker. Garlunk had been asleep for a hundred and two years, seven months and three days. He stood up, and the beard fell like a waterfall. It tumbled down his whole long length, then lay in a matted heap at his feet. It was a huge puddle of hair.

It went from yellow to ginger to brown to black. It was as if it had got bored, just slowly growing in that silent cave. So every few years it had grown a different colour, just for a change. It wasn't exactly a rainbow of a beard (there was no green, for instance) but it was certainly colourful.

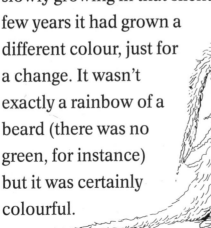

"Botheration beard!" Garlunk growled, and again the people below thought they heard thunder. "Where's my shears?"

These were the sheep shears he had stolen long ago. First he had eaten the shepherd, then stolen his shears.

Garlunk peered back into the gloomy cave. He could not see the shears. He got down on his hands and knees. He crawled about the cave among the littered bones and skulls. Even then the beard got in the way. It kept getting trapped under his knees.

Having your beard tugged is no joke. It hurts. "Ouch!" roared Garlunk.

"OUCH!"

TWO

NOW someone else comes into the story. Her name is Poppy, and she is eight years, three months and four days old. She goes to Witherspoon Road Primary School. She has fair hair and blue eyes – but that isn't important.

What *is* important is that she likes adventure and excitement. She wishes that real life was more like an adventure in a book. (Poppy always has her nose in a book. She says it is the best place in the world for any nose to be.)

In real life, people eat cornflakes and

fish fingers. (Not at the same time, of course.) They go for walks and clean cars and watch television.

In books, people eat peacock pies and talk to fairies who can grant wishes, they chase pirates and meet men from the moon.

Poppy wishes that something like that would happen to her. She'd better look out.

At just about the time when Garlunk was waking from his long sleep, Poppy's family were about to set off for Wales. They were going not to the seaside, but to a cottage in the mountains.

Poppy liked the seaside. She didn't think this holiday sounded much of an adventure. "I think it's silly, a place being called Wales when there aren't any whales there," she said.

"And you're silly if you think whales live up mountains," said Joe. He was her

brother, and had been ten last week. He went round boasting that now he was in double figures.

"Ah," said Dad, "but there are dragons in Wales."

Poppy cheered up. This sounded more like it. "What – breathing fire?"

Poppy could see one already in her mind's eye. It had green shiny scales and was nearly as long as an Intercity train.

"Green eyes, breathing fire and all!" said Dad.

"*Man*-eating dragons?"

"You never know what you'll find in Wales," Dad went on. "Dragons, wizards, caves and giants!"

"Oh stop!" Now Poppy was dizzy. Her head was full of pictures.

"I don't believe in dragons," Joe said. "Or giants."

"Oh *you*!" said Poppy. "Just because you're in double figures! You don't believe in anything any more!"

"I just hope Clutterbuck doesn't see any dragons, that's all," Joe said. "He'd have a fit."

Clutterbuck was slumped by the door with his nose on his paws. He was white with black splodges, and not very brave. Dad said he thought he could be a mouse in disguise.

"Clutterbuck will love Wales," Mum said. "Dragons or no dragons, giants or no giants."

"Time to get the car packed," Dad said.

So they packed the car, then got in and drove off. They went for miles and miles and miles.

Then they saw the mountains ahead – blue, misty and magical. And at last, there was the cottage, built of grey stone and with purple hollyhocks by the door.

As soon as the car drew up, Poppy flew out of the door.

All around, the grass was littered with rocks and stones as old as the hills. Some of the bigger ones were dragon-shaped. Some of them even seemed to have faces.

"They could be dragons turned into stone," she thought. "Perhaps if someone says the magic word, they change back into dragons!"

She tried out a few magic words like abracadabra, but nothing happened. She made a few up. "Stitherup!" she said. "Ticktackallyack! Boomerangtiffilop!"

Nothing. (Perhaps you know some better ones?)

"Pity I don't speak Welsh," said Poppy to Clutterbuck. "I bet you have to say it in Welsh!"

She looked up again at the mountain. "The mountain where giants live!" thought Poppy.

She had always wanted to meet a giant. She wanted to ask one how he managed to find clothes to fit, and what he used to brush his teeth. She wanted to see a giant's knife and fork, which would be as big as garden tools. A giant's teacup must be as big as a bucket, and his boots the size of a rowing boat.

Poppy forgot that giants quite often make snacks of small girls and boys. She forgot that they have long yellow teeth, all the better to eat with. Poppy forgot that so far she had met giants only in fairy tales.

Fairy tales have happy endings. Life isn't always like that.

THREE

GARLUNK didn't have many brains. He was all beard and teeth. He was hungry. He couldn't go down the mountain and catch a sheep because his beard tripped him up. He had forgotten where he had put his shears. (To be fair, there is no wonder. A hundred and two years, seven months and three days is rather a long time to remember anything.)

If he didn't eat soon, he would starve. What was he to do?

What would *you* do,
if your beard had grown
and grown and grown until
you couldn't move without
tripping over it? Think about
it. Work it out. Remember
that you have no shears and
no scissors.

I expect you've already got
the answer, but I'll tell you.

You would wind that beard
round and round your waist,
like a sash, then tuck in
the end.

Or you could wind it round
and round your neck, like a scarf.
Then off you'd go.

Garlunk didn't think of that. Oh
no. The answers he thought of were
no use at all. The first thing he
thought was, "If I can't go out and
catch food, I shall have to stop *here*
and catch it."

So Garlunk sat in the mouth
of his cave and waited for birds
to fly past. So they did – buzzards
and hawks and kites. Out went
his huge fist to snatch them as
they flew. Snatch! Snatch!

He didn't so much as touch
a feather. Lucky for them. If he
had caught a bird, he would have

stuffed it straight into his mouth, feathers, beak and all.

It was hopeless.

When Garlunk realised that he wasn't going to catch a bird even if he sat there for *another* hundred and two years, seven months and three days, he began to blub.

Like most big bullies, he wasn't very brave. "Boo hoo hoo! I shall die, I shall die!"

A little stream of giant's tears began to splash down the mountainside. Then it grew to a river, then a flood.

The silly sheep ran out of its way, frightened that they would drown. Far above, Garlunk heard their bleats, and the sound made him hungrier than ever. That sound was like the sound of sausages sizzling in a pan would be to you and me.

Garlunk stopped crying. He took out a handkerchief the size of a table-cloth and wiped his eyes.

"Think!" He banged his own head with his fist – bang, bang!

"THINK!"

He had another idea. It was a terrible one, even worse than the first. "What I'll do is pull my beard out, hair by hair!"

"OUCH!"

Would *you* like to pull your own beard out, hair by hair? If you don't have a beard, try to imagine pulling your own hair out. And Garlunk, remember, was even more of a cowardy custard than most of us.

He took a deep breath, squeezed his eyes tight shut, and took hold of a hair . . .

The people in the valley below thought the storm was getting nearer. Most of them had forgotten that their grandparents said there was a giant living up there on the mountain.

And some of them, of course, had only just arrived, on holiday.

"That sounded like thunder," Joe said.

"Doesn't look like rain," Poppy said. "Tell Dad I've gone to explore."

She was going to be a proper explorer. She took an apple, a bag of crisps, her special knife with five attachments, and a mirror. She held up the mirror to catch the light. The sun struck it and made it blaze.

"If I'm in danger, I shall flash a signal with the mirror," Poppy said. "SOS."

"As long as the sun doesn't go in," Joe said.

Poppy stuck her tongue out at him.

"Go on," he said. "Let's see you do SOS."

So Poppy tilted the glass till it caught the sun. She didn't know all the morse code, but she did know SOS: *dot dot dot, dash dash dash, dot dot dot*.

"You'd better take Clutterbuck," Joe said, "though I expect he'd run a mile if he saw a dragon or a giant. If there *were* such things."

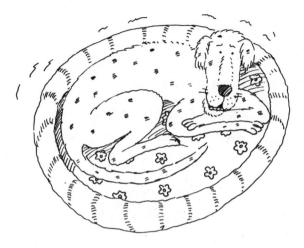

Just then there was another rumble of thunder.

This, if they had only known it, was Garlunk's yell of delight. He had given up pulling his beard out hair by hair. Now he had the best idea of all. (Or worst.)

"I can't walk down the mountain – so I'll roly-poly down!" He thought it was probably the best idea he had ever had in his whole life.

He lay down and put both his arms straight down by his sides. Then he shut his eyes.

Most people might think it silly to go roly-polying down a rocky mountainside with their eyes shut. But Garlunk didn't dare risk keeping his eyes open. Remember the wizard, and the curse!

With his eyes open, Garlunk might perhaps catch sight of himself in a pool or even a puddle. If he did, he would turn to stone, and that was his worst nightmare.

He shut his eyes, tight, took a deep breath . . . and started to roll.

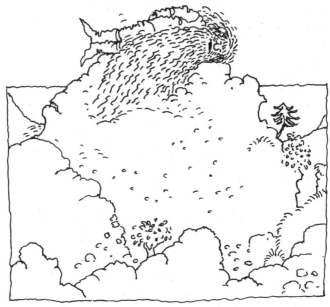

FOUR

NOW the two parts of our story come together.

Poppy and Clutterbuck are climbing up the mountain, and Garlunk is roly-polying down it. If Poppy doesn't look out, she'll be squashed as flat as a pancake, and that will be the end of her.

Clutterbuck kept very close to her. He didn't much like the look of the sheep. They looked dangerous. He was big, but they were bigger. (And Garlunk, of course, was bigger than the whole lot of them put together.)

As they climbed higher up the mountainside, there were more and more rocks.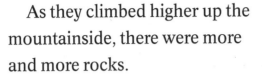

Poppy peered behind each one to make sure a dragon wasn't hiding there. Some of them were huge. She would come back and climb one, she thought, when she had finished meeting giants and dragons.

Wheeee!

There came a strange roar. Poppy had never heard such a sound in her life.

Wheeee!

Clutterbuck stopped dead and
pricked up his ears. Poppy looked up
and saw what looked like an enormous
tree-trunk rolling down the mountain.

"Quick!" She ran behind
a rock and Clutterbuck shot
after her.

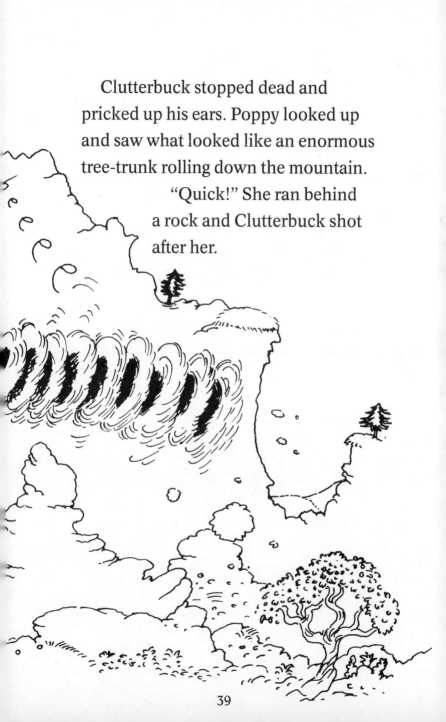

Garlunk was roly-polying down the mountainside and couldn't stop. He hadn't thought of that. (I told you he hadn't many brains.)

Faster and faster he went, whizzing over and over, then – WHAM! – he had hit a rock. It was the rock Poppy and Clutterbuck were hiding behind.

Garlunk tried to get up. He couldn't. What was more, he couldn't move his arms or legs.

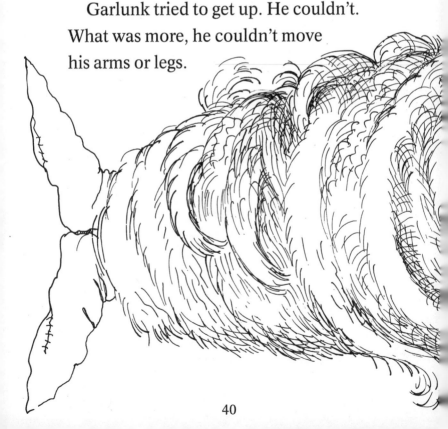

As he rolled, his beard had wound itself round and round him. Now he was bandaged in it from head to toe, like a mummy.

He hadn't thought of that, either. He was worse off now than he had been before. He did not even know where he was, because his eyes were still tight shut.

"I'm done for!" he thought. "I'm going to be the first giant in the history of the world to die wound up in his own beard!"

It was a terrible thought. He was tempted to start crying again.

He lay there wondering whether perhaps he could roly-poly back *up* the mountain, back to his own cave. Then he might be able to find his shears, and free himself. (Have *you* ever tried roly-polying up a mountain?)

Poppy and Clutterbuck crouched on the other side of the rock. Clutterbuck's nose was working overtime, and now Poppy too could smell a horrible smell. She had never known a pong like it, having never before met a giant who has not washed for hundreds of years.

Slowly, very slowly, she peered round the rock. She stared. She had never seen anything like it in her life. Was it a tree-trunk? If so, it was a very hairy one.

Clutterbuck ran forward, sniffed, then ran back again. He stood there, growling.

Poppy walked to one end of it. And then she saw the face! She saw a knobby nose and a huge mouth – but no eyes!

"Help!" said Poppy.

"Who's that?" growled Garlunk.

Poppy nearly jumped out of her skin. "It's me – Poppy. Why don't you open your eyes?"

"Where am I? Is there a pool about? Is there a pool or a lake or puddle?"

"No," said Poppy, puzzled. She did not know about the curse. "There's just me and Clutterbuck."

Then, carefully, just squinting at first, the piggy eyes opened.

Garlunk saw Poppy. He saw his dinner –
a lovely juicy little girl and an interesting-
looking spotted sheep. His mouth
watered.

"Help!" he said.

That was when Poppy saw his great
yellow teeth, as big as tombstones. Then
she knew for sure. "A giant!" she said,
and even then didn't have the sense to
be scared, as you and I would have been.

Clutterbuck took a
mouthful of Garlunk's
beard and tugged it.

"Help!" said Garlunk again. "I'm dying. I'm dying of hunger. I haven't eaten a thing for a hundred and two years, seven months and three days." (Don't ask me how he knew how long he had slept. I don't know.)

This sounded a very long time to Poppy. She thought that even four hours between meals was too long.

"Here," she said. "Open your mouth!"

The giant obeyed. Poppy leaned over and threw her apple into the great red cave of his mouth. It snapped shut.

"What was that?" asked Garlunk. "A gnat?"

Poppy went right up close. She did not even notice that Clutterbuck was whimpering and whining.

"Open wide!" she said again.

48

The giant obeyed. Poppy shook the bag of crisps down his throat in a shower. He gulped and coughed as they hit his tonsils.

"What was that?" he asked. "Feathers?"

"I'm afraid that's all the food I've got," Poppy told him.

The giant looked longingly at the dalmatian. "Could you just pass me that sheep, to be going on with?" he asked. "That spotted one."

"That's Clutterbuck," Poppy said. "And you're not having him. Where are your arms and legs? And what's all that fur?"

"It's my beard," he told her. "The dratted thing's wound itself round me. Do something, can't you?"

He did not speak very politely. Some people would have walked off and left him to unravel himself.

But Poppy was delighted to meet a giant at last. She remembered her special knife with five attachments. She took it from her pocket and opened it.

"Hurray!" shouted Garlunk. "Cut me free!"

"Wait a minute," said Poppy, who was not stupid. "If I do, how do I know you won't eat me?"

"As if I would!" said Garlunk. "The very idea!"

"You've got to promise not to," Poppy told him.

"Promise!" said Garlunk.

He did not even know the meaning of the word. The minute Poppy had cut him free, he meant to gobble her up, in double quick time.

Have you ever known a giant keep a promise?

FIVE

POPPY decided to start at the giant's feet and work her way up. His boots were just poking through the beard. She climbed up, pulling herself by the long hairs. Close up, the pong was horrible, but she was too polite to mention it.

"This is amazing!" she said. "I didn't know there was so much hair in the whole world!"

She was in a forest of hair, a jungle. She saw it stretch on and on. It went from yellow to ginger to brown to black.

"Why is it all different colours?" she asked.

"Because it gets bored growing all one colour," Garlunk replied. "And I'm getting bored, waiting for my dinner. Get cutting, can't you?"

You might have thought he would mind his manners if he wanted Poppy to do him a favour. But giants don't know the meaning of the word 'manners'.

Poppy started to cut.

Clutterbuck danced and barked. "Don't!" he was saying. "Don't, don't, don't!" But to Poppy it just sounded like barking.

It was hard work. It was more like cutting wire than hair. Up and up she went.

First Garlunk's feet were free, then his knees, then his whole legs. "That's better!" he said.

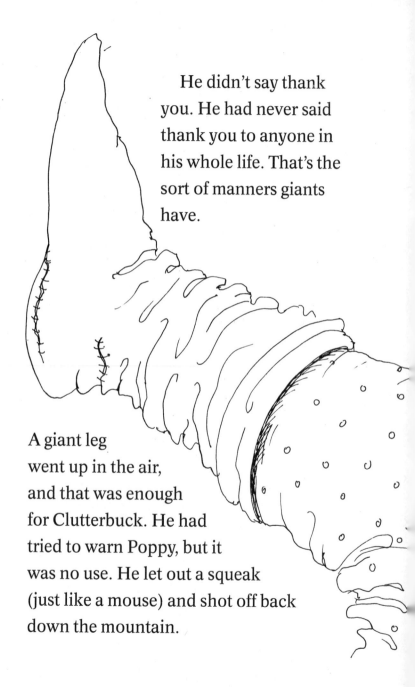

He didn't say thank you. He had never said thank you to anyone in his whole life. That's the sort of manners giants have.

A giant leg went up in the air, and that was enough for Clutterbuck. He had tried to warn Poppy, but it was no use. He let out a squeak (just like a mouse) and shot off back down the mountain.

"Now look what you've done!" Poppy said. "You've frightened Clutterbuck!"

"Pity," said Garlunk. What he meant was that it was a pity he had lost such a tasty-looking snack. He had never eaten a spotted sheep before.

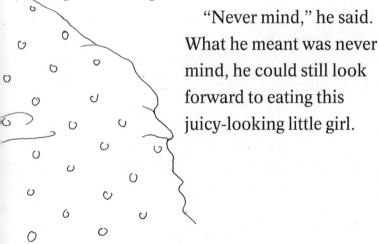

"Never mind," he said. What he meant was never mind, he could still look forward to eating this juicy-looking little girl.

Poppy sawed and hacked away at the beard. It was hot in all that hair, and smelly, and her arms were getting tired.

Now the giant's hands were free, now his elbows, and now his whole arms.

"Got you!"

Poppy let out a scream.

Garlunk's huge fingers went round her and he lifted her up with one hand. With the other he pushed himself up so that he was sitting upright. "Dinner time!" he roared.

"No! No! You promised!"

Poor Poppy. She really should have known better than to trust a giant's promise.

It was rather late in the day to signal
SOS. But she snatched her mirror from
her pocket anyway, and held it up to
where she hoped the sun was.

Above her Poppy saw that great red cave with its yellow tombstones.

"Goodbye, world!" she cried. "Oh help – SOS!"

That was when Garlunk made his mistake. He looked down at his dinner, and caught sight of one of his own piggy eyes in the mirror.

"OOOOOEEEEEEEECH!"

The people down in the valley had never heard thunder like it, and never would again. The wizard's curse was working.

One minute Poppy was on her way into a giant's mouth, the next she found herself on top of a huge rock.

She looked down. The ground was a very long way off. She was no longer about to be a giant's dinner, but she was still in a fix. How would she ever get down?

The mirror was still in her hand. (Little did she know that it had already saved her life.)

"Help! SOS!"

Then Clutterbuck was there, then Mum and Dad and Joe. "Oh Poppy!" said Mum. "However did you get up there?"

"I didn't! A giant did it!"

"What a fib!" said Joe. "You've got giants on the brain."

Poppy stuck her tongue out at him.

"We could do with a ladder," Mum said.

But Dad was already climbing. He was groping for toe and finger holds, and little did he know he was scaling a stone giant.

Poppy held her breath. What if the giant changed back when Dad was only half-way up? She still had her eyes squeezed tight when she felt him lift her.

"Giant, my foot!" said Joe, when they were safely down.

"I know it doesn't look much like one," Poppy said, "but that's because of his beard. There was miles and miles of it and it went from yellow to ginger to brown to black, and I was cutting it with my special knife and he *promised* not to eat me, and then – "

She stopped. They were looking at her, all three. She could tell by their faces that they didn't believe a single word she was saying.

"Oh well!" said Poppy. "Never mind. Anyway, I can cross giants off my list now. Tomorrow . . . it's dragons!"

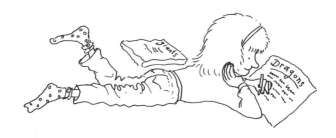